3 2148 00148 8880

CLARK THE SHARK

WRITTEN BY **BRUCE HALE**   ILLUSTRATED BY **GUY FRANCIS**

HARPER

An Imprint of HarperCollins Publishers

To Grannie Annie, with love
—B.H.

To Max and Mattie
—G.F.

Library of Congress Cataloging-in-Publication Data
Hale, Bruce.
  Clark the Shark / written by Bruce Hale ; illustrated by Guy Francis. — 1st ed.
    p. cm.
  Summary: Clark finds everything about school fun and exciting, but his enthusiasm
causes problems until he begins inventing rhymes to remind himself to stay cool at
school.
  ISBN 978-0-06-219226-4 (hardcover bdgs)
  [1. Schools—Fiction. 2. Behavior—Fiction. 3. Sharks—Fiction. 4. Marine animals—Fiction.]
I. Francis, Guy, ill. II. Title.
PZ7.H1295Cl 2013   2012030234
[E]—dc23   CIP
                                                                AC

Book design by John Sazaklis

13 14 15 16 17 SCP 10 9 8 7 6 5 4 3 2 1
❖
First Edition

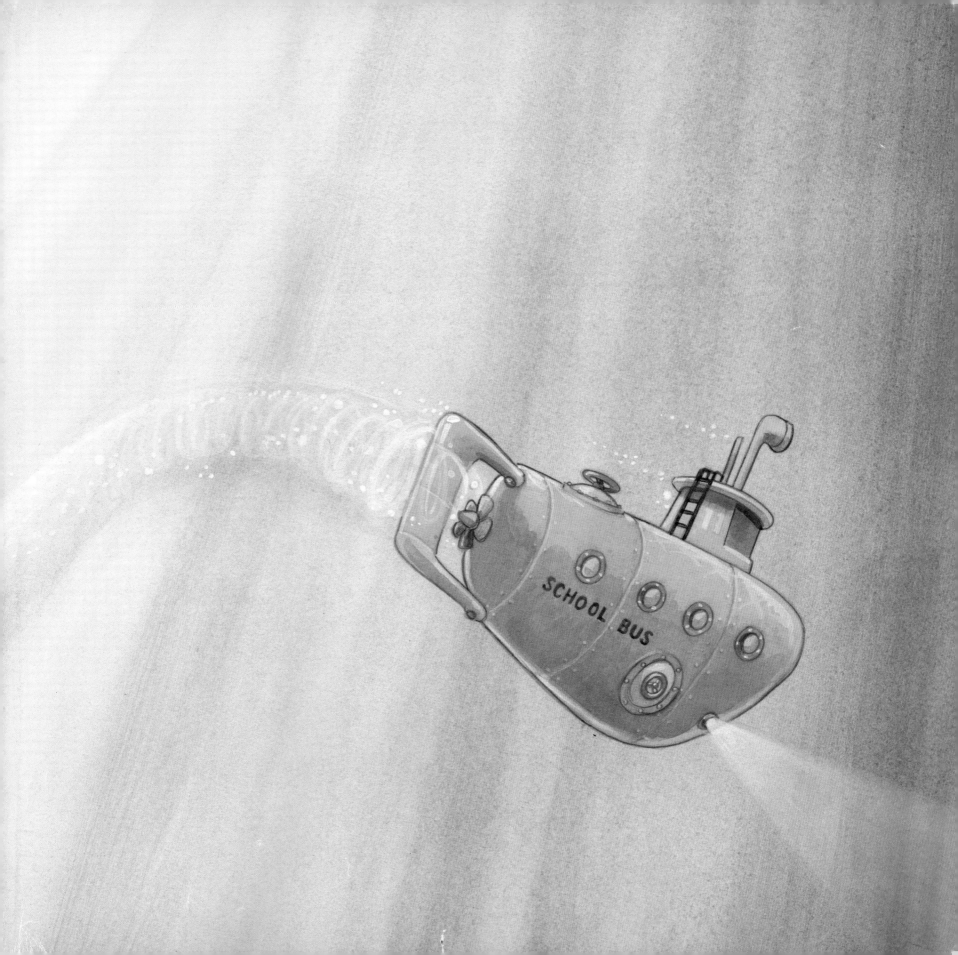

In all the wide blue seas, in all the wide blue world, the top school for fish was Theodore Roosterfish Elementary. And of all the fish at Theodore Roosterfish, the biggest and the strongest was Clark the Shark.

Clark loved school, and he loved his teacher, Mrs. Inkydink. He loved to play upsy-downsy and spinna-ma-jig with his friends. Clark *loved* his life.

"SCHOOL IS AWESOME!" shouted Clark the Shark.
"Less shouting, more reading,"
said Mrs. Inkydink.

"LUNCHTIME IS SWEEEEET!" yelled Clark the Shark.

"Munch your *own* lunch," said his best friend, Joey Mackerel.

"RECESS ROCKS!" bellowed Clark the Shark.

"You are playing rough, Clark!" cried the other kids.

Yes, Clark loved his life with all of his sharky heart. But he loved everything *way* too much.

He was too loud.

He was too wild.

He was just too much shark for the other fish to handle.

After a while, no one would play with Clark. No one ate lunch with him. No one sat with him at circle time. Even his best friend, Joey Mackerel, said, "Cool your jets, Clark! You're making me crazy!"

One day, Clark asked Mrs. Inkydink, "What's *wrong* with everyone?"

Mrs. Inkydink patted his fin. "Clark, sometimes you play too hard, you munch too hard, and—gosh—you even help too hard."

"But life is SO exciting!" said Clark.

"There's a time and a place for everything," said
Mrs. Inkydink. "And sometimes the rule is *stay cool.*"

STAY
COOL!

At recess, Clark tried to stay cool, but he pushed the
swing with too much zing! "Sorry," said Clark. "I forgot."
"Yikes!" cried Joey Mackerel.

At lunch, Clark tried to stay cool, but everything smelled so good that he munched a bunch of lunches.

"Sorry," said Clark. "I forgot."

"We're STARVING!" said his friends.

In class, Clark tried to stay cool, but a good book got him all shook up.

"Now, Clark!" said Mrs. Inkydink. "This isn't the time or the place. Tell me, what's the rule?"

"Stay cool," said Clark.

"Hey, that rhymes!" he cried.

Then Clark got a big idea in his sharky head. *Maybe if I make a rhyme, I'll remember every time!* he thought. The next day, he put his plan to work.

In class, when lessons got exciting, Clark wanted to bounce up out of his seat.

Instead, he told himself: "When teacher's talking, don't go walking."

And what do you know? It worked!

"Attaboy, Clark!" said Mrs. Inkydink.

Clark smiled. "Lessons are fun!"

At lunch, everything smelled *sooo* yummy. When Clark wanted to eat and eat and never stop, he told himself: "Only munch your own lunch."

And it worked again!

"Way to go, Clark!" said his friends.

Clark grinned. "Lunch is fun."

At playtime, Clark told himself: "Easy does it, that's the way.

"Then my friends will let me play."

And playtime was fun. Once more, Clark loved his life.

But then a shadow fell across the playground—a *gi-normous* shadow with tentacles galore. "It's a new kid, and he looks scary!" cried Joey Mackerel. "Swim for your lives!"

The squid squashed the slide, and it snapped off the swings.

"Oops. My bad," said the new kid.

"Wait," said Clark. "He just wants to play. Let's find a way!"

And he swam at the new kid with all his might. Clark played harder than he ever had before—upsy-downsy and spinna-ma-jig.

Why, he even made up a new game: tail-whump-a-lumpus!

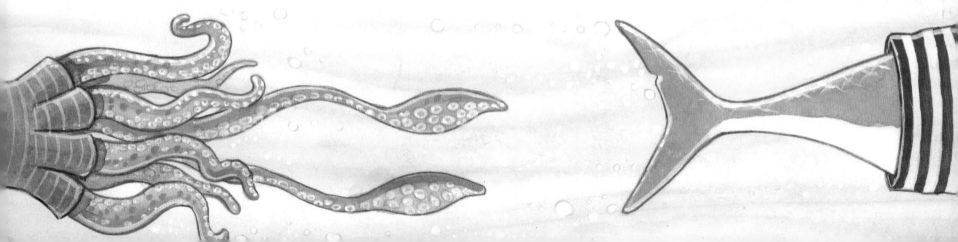

"Wow, that was fun," said the new kid breathlessly, and he settled down.
"If you want to come to school, you've got to stay cool," said Clark.

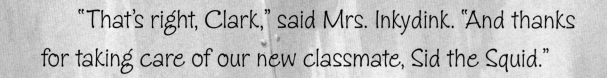

"That's right, Clark," said Mrs. Inkydink. "And thanks
for taking care of our new classmate, Sid the Squid."

"Hooray for Clark the Shark!"
everyone cheered.

That night Clark's mother asked, "What did you learn at school, dear?"
"There's a time and a place for everything," Clark said. "Sometimes you stay cool."

"But sometimes a shark's gotta do what a shark's gotta do."